THE SHERLOCK HOLMES

CHILDREN'S COLLECTION

CREATURES, CODES AND CURIOUS CASES

Published by Sweet Cherry Publishing Limited
Unit 36, Vulcan House,
Vulcan Road,
Leicester, LE5 3EF
United Kingdom

First published in the UK in 2021
2021 edition

2 4 6 8 10 9 7 5 3

ISBN: 978-1-78226-439-2

Sherlock Holmes: The Second Stain

Cover design by Arianna Bellucci and Amy Booth
Illustrations by Arianna Bellucci

Lexile® code numerical measure L = Lexile® 680L

www.sweetcherrypublishing.com

Printed and bound in China
C.WM004

SHERLOCK HOLMES

THE SECOND STAIN

SIR ARTHUR CONAN DOYLE

Sweet Cherry

Chapter One

One Tuesday morning, Mrs Hudson showed two gentlemen up to our rooms in Baker Street. Her eyes were wide as she led them in.

I was surprised to recognise the famous face of Lord Bellinger, the prime minister. He had a serious look and sharp eyes. The other man had dark hair and an elegant appearance. He was Mr Trelawney Hope, the foreign minister.

I took their coats, my hands shaking a little with nerves.

'Please sit down, gentlemen,' said Holmes, pointing to a sofa strewn with papers. They did so, and it was clear from their anxious faces that a very serious case had brought them here. The prime minister's thin, blue-veined hands were clasped tightly over the handle of his umbrella. His face looked gloomily from Holmes to me and back again.

The foreign minister pulled nervously at his moustache and fidgeted with his watch chain. It was he who spoke first. 'Mr Holmes,' he began. 'At eight o'clock this morning I discovered that an important document

has gone missing. I told the prime minister at once and he suggested coming to you.'

'Have you told the police?' asked Holmes, as we both sat down facing them.

'No,' the prime minister said sharply. 'We have not, and we must not. I cannot trust that every police officer working on the case would keep the document a secret. And it *must* be kept a secret.'

'And why is that, sir?' asked Holmes.

'Because the lost document is extremely important. If it were read by the wrong people, it could lead to war. Unless it can be recovered in secret, it may as well not be recovered at all,' the prime minister explained.

Holmes nodded. 'I understand. Now, Mr Hope, please tell me exactly how the document disappeared.'

'That can be done in a few words, Mr Holmes,' said Mr Hope. 'It was a letter from a very powerful and important person in Europe. We received it six days ago. It was so important that I didn't even keep it in my safe. I carried the letter with me every day from the Houses of Parliament to my house in Whitehall Terrace, where it was locked in a box in my bedroom. I am certain that it was there last night because I opened the box while I was dressing for dinner and I saw the letter inside.

Yet this morning it was gone.

'The box didn't move from my bedside table all night; it sat right next to my glass of water. I am a light sleeper and so is my wife. No one could have entered the room during the night without waking us. And yet, somehow, the letter disappeared.'

'What time did you have dinner?' asked Holmes.

'Half-past seven,' said Mr Hope.

'And what time did you go to bed?' asked Holmes.

'My wife had gone to the theatre,' said Mr Hope, glancing

up at ceiling as he tried to remember the details. 'I waited up for her. It was about half-past eleven when we went to bed.'

'So for four hours the box was unguarded?' said Holmes.

'Well, yes,' Mr Hope said, 'but no one is ever allowed into my bedroom except my butler or my wife's maid during the day. They are both trusty servants, who have been with us for a long time. Besides, neither of them could possibly have known that there was anything more than ordinary papers in the box. No one in the house knew about the document.'

Holmes raised his eyebrows. 'Surely your wife knew?'

'No, sir,' said Mr Hope. 'I had said nothing to my wife about the letter until it went missing this morning.'

The prime minister patted Mr Hope on the shoulder. 'I know how trustworthy you are,' he said, 'and I'm sure you were extremely careful in this case.'

Mr Hope nodded keenly.

'Have you lost any documents before?' asked Holmes.

Mr Hope shook his head. 'No, sir.'

'Who is there in England who knows about the letter?' asked Holmes.

'Every member of the Cabinet was told about it yesterday. But they were sworn to secrecy by the prime minister. I cannot imagine that any of them would have broken that promise. Good heavens! To think that in a few hours I lost it!'

Mr Hope's handsome face fell and he covered his eyes with his hands. For a moment we could see the real man rather than the serious, stern version of him that was so regularly smeared across

Cabinet

A Cabinet is a team of the most high-ranking state officials and politicians in the United Kingdom. Each person is chosen by the Prime Minister to be in charge of a different department, such as transport, health and hospitals, educations and schools, and environment. That person can then help decide which laws and policies should affect their department. Cabinet members meet regularly to discuss important and sometimes secret matters of government.

the morning newspapers. Then, as suddenly as it appeared, it was gone, and Mr Hope returned to being a solemn politician.

'Besides the members of the Cabinet, there are perhaps two or three officials who know about the letter,' he said. 'No one else in England knows, Mr Holmes, I assure you.'

'But abroad?' asked Holmes.

'Only the man who wrote it,' said Mr Hope.

Holmes thought about it for some time before saying: 'I must ask you exactly what was in that letter and why its disappearance could be so disastrous.'

Our two guests looked at each other. The prime minister's shaggy eyebrows gathered in a frown.

'Mr Holmes,' the prime minister said, 'the envelope is long, thin and blue. On the back there is a seal of red wax, stamped with a crouching lion.

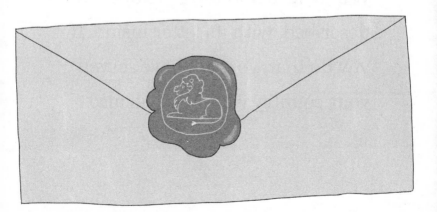

It is addressed in large scrawling handwriting to–'

Holmes interrupted him. 'That is very interesting and useful information, Prime Minister, but what was *written* in the letter?'

'That is a State secret. I cannot tell you,' said the prime minister. 'I don't think it's important, anyway. I have been told that you possess great deductive powers. All I need you to do is find the envelope I've described, with its letter inside. If you do that, you will have served your country well. You will also have earned any reward that we can offer you.'

Holmes got to his feet with a smile.

'I am sorry, but I can't help you in this matter,' he said. 'You are both very busy men, and I am too. I don't want to waste your time, so you'd best leave.'

Chapter Two

The prime minster sprang to his feet with the same fierce gleam in his eyes that usually made his Cabinet members cower.

'I am not used to being treated …' he began, before taking a deep breath and slowly lowering himself back onto the sofa.

For a moment we all sat in silence. Then the prime minister

shrugged his shoulders and started to speak again. 'We must accept your terms, Mr Holmes. You are probably right: it is not fair that we should ask for your help and not tell you everything.

'You and Doctor Watson must both promise never to tell anyone what you're about to hear. If you did, you would be betraying your country and putting us all into great danger.'

'You can trust us,' said Holmes, and I nodded.

'The letter is from a powerful

foreign king,' said the prime minister. 'Something happened between us that upset him and he wrote a very rude and insulting letter to me.'

Holmes wrote a name on a piece of paper and handed it to the prime minister, who nodded. 'You're correct – it was him. He wrote the letter.'

I was amazed. I had no idea how Holmes could have guessed who wrote the letter. I leaned forwards, desperate to know the name of this troublemaking king,

but the prime minister simply
smiled at me and tucked the
paper into his jacket pocket.

'Have you told this man that it's
missing?' asked Holmes.

'Yes, sir, we sent a telegram in code,' said Mr Hope.

'Perhaps he *wants* the letter to be read,' suggested Holmes.

'No. We think that he already regrets sending it,' said Mr Hope. 'It would cause more trouble to him and his country if the contents of the letter were revealed.'

'Then why would anyone steal it?'

'Mr Holmes,' said the prime minister, 'the whole of Europe is divided in two at the moment, with powerful countries on both sides and Britain in the middle. Both sides want Britain to join their team. If this letter were to start a war between Britain and side A, then we would have to join forces with side B. Hence, side B would become stronger.'

'So if the enemies of this powerful person – the people on "side B", as you call it – got hold of the letter, it would cause a war not only between us and the person who wrote it, but an entire world war?' asked Holmes.

'Yes, sir,' said Mr Hope.

'So where do you think this missing letter has been sent?' asked Holmes.

The prime minster replied, 'It could have been sent to any agent or government in Europe. It is probably on its way right now, travelling as fast as steam power can take it.'

Mr Hope dropped his head on his chest and groaned.

The prime minister put a

hand on his shoulder. 'It was just bad luck, my dear fellow. No one can blame you. You took every precaution. Now, Mr Holmes, you know all the facts. What do you think we should do?'

Holmes shook his head sadly. 'You think that unless this document is found there will be war?'

'It's very likely,' said the prime minster.

'Then, sir, we must prepare for war.'

Chapter Three

Holmes' words weighed heavily on us all.

'Think of the facts, sir,' said Holmes. 'The letter couldn't have been taken after eleven-thirty last night, because Mr Hope and his wife were both in the room from then until the loss was discovered. No one would have been able to sneak in and steal it without waking them up. It was therefore taken between seven-thirty and eleven-thirty. It was probably early on, because whoever took it would want to get it as soon as possible.'

The two men nodded.

'Now, sir,' Holmes continued, 'if the important document was taken at around seven-thirty last night, where is it now? Let's think: the thief would have wanted to send it on quickly. And there are hundreds of different agents and governments it could have been sent to. So what chance do we have now of finding it? Almost none at all.'

Holmes' words sent a shiver of fear down my spine.

The prime minister got up from the sofa and began pacing. 'What you say is perfectly logical, Mr Holmes. But surely there must be *something* we can do? Some way to trace the letter?'

'Well, let us say that the letter was taken by the maid or the butler,' Holmes suggested.

Mr Hope shook his head. 'They are trusted staff!'

Holmes tutted and turned to Mr Hope. 'I understand that your room is on the second floor, Mr Hope? And that there is no way of getting in from outside?'

Mr Hope nodded.

'Nor could anyone come in through the bedroom door without being seen?' said Holmes.

Mr Hope nodded again.

'It must then be someone in the house who has taken it,' Holmes said. 'But which international spy would they have taken it to? There are three who live in London,

who spring to mind. I will begin
by checking that they are all still
in the city. If one is missing –
especially if he has been missing
since last night – we will have some
idea of where the letter has gone.'

'Why would he be missing?'
asked Mr Hope. 'Surely he would
take the letter to his country's
embassy in London.'

'I don't think so,' said
Holmes. 'These agents work for
themselves.'

The prime minister nodded in
agreement. 'I think you are right,

Mr Holmes. An agent would not give away such a valuable item. He would want to sell it to the highest bidder. I think your plan

Embassy

There are several embassies in London, each owned by a different country. They are buildings where the ambassador (the representative of that country) can work and sometimes live. An embassy looks after its citizens when they are living abroad – for instance, if an American person came to England and then fell ill or became the victim of a serious crime, the American embassy in London could help them. The ambassador, who works in the embassy, will also help manage the relationship between England and their own country.

is an excellent one.' He turned to the Foreign Minister. 'Meanwhile, Mr Hope, we have work to do. We cannot sit here all day feeling sorry for ourselves.'

I helped the gentlemen with their coats and they turned to the door.

'If anything else happens during the day, we shall let you know, Mr Holmes,' said the prime minister. 'And I hope you will let us know the results of your enquiries?'

'Certainly, Prime Minister,' said Holmes, with a small bow.

When our visitors had left,

Holmes lit a pipe and returned to his armchair. I sat down too and picked up the morning paper.

I was reading a fascinating article about a murder that had happened the night before, when Holmes suddenly sprang to his feet.

'Yes!' he cried, placing his pipe on the shelf above the fireplace. 'There is no better way of doing it. I was being too negative before – the situation is desperate but not hopeless. If we could find out which spy has taken the letter, it might just be possible that they still have it.'

'Do you really think so, Holmes?' I asked.

'I'm not sure, but I hope so. These fellows are only interested in money, you see. Whichever spy has the letter will currently be getting lots of offers from all over the world to buy it off him. The longer he holds on to the letter, the more money the countries will offer. So it's possible that he may still have it with him.' Holmes tapped his fingers against his chin, thinking.

'The three spies I suspect are: Oberstein, La Rothière, and

Eduardo Lucas. I will go to see each of them.'

I glanced back at the newspaper. 'Is that Eduardo Lucas of Godolphin Street?'

'Yes.'

'You will not see him,' I said.

'Why not?' Holmes replied, sounding slightly annoyed.

'It says here that he was murdered in his house last night,' I said.

Holmes stared in amazement and then snatched the paper from my hands.

The Times

Tuesday, 16th October 1894

MURDER IN WESTMINSTER

A mysterious murder was committed last night in Godolphin Street, in the shadow of the Houses of Parliament. The victim, Mr Eduardo Lucas, was well known for his charming personality and his wonderful singing voice. Mr Lucas was thirty-four years old and unmarried. He lived with his housekeeper and his butler. Last night the housekeeper went to bed early in her bedroom in the attic, and the butler was out for the evening. At quarter to twelve, Police Constable Barrett was passing through Godolphin Street when he noticed that the front door of number sixteen – Mr Lucas' home – was open. He saw that there was a light on in the sitting room so he knocked at the door. When no one answered, he went in. The sitting

room was
a terrible
mess.
All the
furniture
had been
pushed
against
the walls,
with just
one chair
lying on its
back in the
middle of
the room.
Next to the
chair, still
grasping
one of its
legs, was
Mr Lucas.
He had been
stabbed
through
the heart
and would
have died
instantly.
The murder
weapon was
a curved
dagger that
had been
plucked
down from
the wall,
where it
had been
displayed
with other
weapons
from around
the world.
Robbery
does not
seem to
have been
the motive
because,
although
the room
contained
valuable
items, none
had been
taken.

'Well, Watson, what do you
make of that?' asked Holmes.

'It's an amazing coincidence,'
I said.

'A coincidence!' said Holmes.
'He is one of the three men who

could have the letter, and he just *happened* to meet a violent death on the same night that the letter was stolen. It's more than a coincidence! No, my dear Watson, the two things *must* be connected. Now we must find the connection.'

Chapter Four

I scratched my head, trying to make sense of the clues we had been given. 'Surely now the police must know about the missing letter?' I said.

Holmes shook his head. 'Not at all,' he said. 'They know about the murder in Godolphin Street, but they don't know anything about what happened in Mr Hope's home. Only we know of both events and can see how they may be linked. There is one obvious link: Godolphin Street, where Mr Lucas lives, is only a few minutes walk from Whitehall Terrace, where Mr Hope lives. The other spies and secret agents I named live on the far side of the West End. It would have been easier for Mr Lucas to receive the letter, being so near. I think it is likely that he's our man.'

There was a knock at the door and Mrs Hudson came in with a visiting card on a silver tray.

Lady Hilda Trelawney Hope
Whitehall Terrace,
Westminster

Holmes glanced at it, raised his eyebrows, and handed it to me.

'Ask Lady Hope to come in please, Mrs Hudson,' said Holmes.

Visiting card
A small card with a person's name and address on it. Sometimes a person will give their visiting card to a servant as a way of introducing themselves before they enter. A card can also be left at a person's house if they are not there when you visit, to let them know you came. A visiting card can also become a key clue for a detective – if a visiting card is found in a crime scene, the detective knows who has been there and where they live, so they can track them down.

A moment later, a beautiful woman entered our apartment. I had often heard her name mentioned and knew that she was the daughter of the Duke of Belminster. As she stepped into the light, I was struck by the look of terror that masked her face.

'Has my husband been here, Mr Holmes?' she asked.

'Yes, madam, he has.'

'Mr Holmes, I beg you not to tell him I was here.'

Holmes showed her a chair. 'Please tell me what I can do for you, but I can't promise not to tell your husband.'

Lady Hope ignored the chair that Holmes had offered and swept across the room in a graceful manner. She looked about for a moment, before sitting in a different chair, with her back to the window.

'Mr Holmes,' she said, her white-gloved hands clasping and unclasping as she spoke. 'I will be honest with you in the hope that you will be honest with me in return. My husband and I have no secrets from each other, except for one thing: politics. He doesn't tell me anything about his work with the prime minister. Now, I know that something terrible happened in our house last night. A paper went missing. But it's political, so my husband won't tell me anything about it.'

Holmes listened, but he didn't nod to confirm what she had said. He had promised to keep the case a secret, and Holmes would never break a promise.

'It is absolutely essential,' went on Lady Hope, 'that I understand what that paper was. I'm sure my husband must have told you all about it. That makes you the only people, apart from the politicians, who know the true facts. I beg you, Mr Holmes, to tell me everything. My husband doesn't realise that he would benefit by me knowing. What was written on that paper?'

'Madam, I cannot tell you,' said Holmes.

Ladt Hope groaned and sank her face into her hands.

'You must see that it is not my place to do so,' said Holmes. 'Your husband told me about the stolen letter in confidence. I cannot go back on my word. And it is not fair of you to ask me. You must ask him to tell you about it himself.'

'I have asked him,' she said. 'You are my last resort. At least tell me this: will my husband's career as a politician be ruined by the loss of this letter?'

Holmes nodded. 'Unless it is found, it could be disastrous,' he said.

She drew in her breath sharply. 'And I understand that there may be even worse consequences for the country?'

'Yes,' said Holmes.

'But what? What consequences?' she asked desperately.

'I cannot tell you,' said Holmes.

'Then I will not take up any more of your time, Mr Holmes,' said Lady Hope, suddenly getting to her feet. 'I beg you not to tell my husband that I came here.'

She walked to the door and then turned to look back at us. Her expression was haunted by

worry as she gave us a final nod goodbye. Then she was gone.

'Now, Watson, you are an expert

on women,' said Holmes with a chuckle, as soon as Lady Hope had gone down the stairs and out of the front door. 'What did she really want?'

'Surely what she said,' I replied. 'She is worried about her husband.'

Holmes tutted. 'No, no, no, Watson. That can't be all. Think of her appearance, her manner, the anxiety bottled up inside her. She was persistent in asking questions.'

'She was certainly worried,' I agreed.

'She said it would benefit her husband if she knew what was in the letter. What did she mean by that? And you must have noticed, Watson, that she chose to sit with her back to the light so that we could not see her expression.'

'Yes,' I said. 'She chose the one chair in the room where she could mask her face.'

'People can be so confusing sometimes, Watson,' said Holmes. 'A very small action may mean a lot, and yet a huge fuss may be made over a small thing.'

Holmes stood up and grabbed his hat and coat. 'Well, goodbye, Watson.'

'You are off?' I asked, surprised.

'Yes, I will spend some time at Godolphin Street with our friends in the police force,' Holmes said. 'The answer to the problem lies with Mr Eduardo Lucas, although I have no idea what that answer could be. Please stay here, my good Watson, and receive any new visitors. I'll join you for lunch if I can.'

Chapter Five

For the next three days Holmes was in a quiet and thoughtful mood. He ran in and out, played short pieces on his violin, regularly sank into daydreams, ate sandwiches at strange hours and hardly answered any of the questions I asked him.

I could tell that things were not
going well with the investigation.
Holmes would not speak about
it, but I managed to find some
information in the newspapers:
Mr Lucas' butler was arrested
and then released. He had an
alibi: he had been visiting friends
that evening and had got home
at midnight. He got on very well
with Mr Lucas and had worked
for him for three years.

The Times

THE EVENING STANDARD

Saturday, 20th October 1894

The Daily

The housekeeper had heard nothing odd or worrying that evening and, to her knowledge, Mr Lucas did not have any visitors.

The room where the murder took place was full of valuable things, but nothing had been stolen. The items showed that Mr Lucas had been interested in politics, speaking other languages and writing letters. He had a lot of friends, but no sweetheart. He had been seen as a respectable man – by those who didn't know that he was a spy, of course – and his death was a complete mystery.

Holmes told me he was in contact with Inspector Lestrade and was being kept up to date with the case.

On the fourth day, an article in the newspaper seemed to solve the whole mystery.

The Daily Telegraph.

Saturday, 20th October 1894

WESTMINSTER MURDERER
FOUND!

The Paris police have made a discovery that is connected to the tragic fate of Mr Eduardo Lucas, who was found stabbed to death on Monday night at his home in Godolphin Street, Westminster. Yesterday, a lady called Madame Henri Fournaye, from Paris, was reported by her servants as being insane. When examined by a doctor, she seemed dangerous and violent. The police discovered that Madame Fournaye had just returned from London. There is evidence to connect her with the crime in Westminster. Photos have shown that Monsieur Henri Fournaye (Madame Fournaye's husband) and Mr Eduardo Lucas are the same person. The man led a double life in London and Paris. Madame Fournaye has always had a terrible temper and has suffered in the past from attacks of jealousy. It is thought that in one of these jealousy-fuelled frenzies she killed her own husband. A woman fitting her description was seen watching Mr Lucas' house in Godolphin Street on Monday night and was then seen again at Charing Cross Station on Tuesday morning, waving her arms about as if in shock. It is thought that jealousy drove Madame Fournaye out of her mind. Doctors say it will be some time before she will be able to answer any questions about the crime.

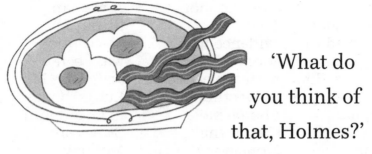

'What do
you think of
that, Holmes?'
I asked, after reading the article
aloud to him while he finished
his breakfast.

Holmes got up from the table
and paced up and down the room.
'My dear Watson, you are very
patient,' he said. 'I have not told
you anything new about the case
for the last three days because
there was nothing new to tell.
Even this newspaper report does
not help much.'

'Surely it answers the question of who killed Mr Lucas?' I said.

'That man's death is a minor problem in comparison to our real task, which is to find the stolen letter and save the country from war.

'Only one important thing has happened in the last three days, Watson, and that is that nothing has happened. I get reports every hour from the government – they've told me that there is no sign of trouble anywhere in Europe. If this letter were loose there would already be signs of trouble – newspaper reports, governments arguing, people rallying their troops. So it can't have been sold to anyone or published anywhere yet.'

Holmes paused to look idly out of the window. Then he turned back to me.

'But if it hasn't been sold to someone in Europe yet, then where is it?' he said. 'Who has it? Why are they hiding it still? That's the question that beats on my brain like a hammer. Did the letter even reach Mr Lucas? If so, why is it not among his papers? Did this wife take it with her after she killed him? If she *did* kill him, that is. And if so, is it in her house in Paris? We cannot search for it there because that would involve the Paris police, and would reveal the secret of the missing letter.'

My head was in a whirl with all the unanswered questions.

'What we need now, Watson, is another clue – something that will help us connect the dots.'

Just then Mrs Hudson came in
and handed Holmes a note.

Holmes,
Something strange at Godolphin
Street.
  Lestrade.

'Put on your hat, Watson. It's
time to go to Godolphin Street,'
said Holmes.

Chapter Six

It was my first visit to the scene of the crime. The house was tall, narrow and very plain. Inspector Lestrade gazed out at us from the front window and greeted us warmly when a constable let us in.

We went into the room where the crime had been committed. The only sign that anything had happened was a stain on the rug

in the centre of the room. Around
it, the floor was made of highly-
polished wood.

Over the fireplace was a magnificent set of weapons. The curved dagger – the weapon used to murder Mr Lucas – was missing.

'Have you seen the article in *The Telegraph*?' asked Inspector Lestrade.

Holmes nodded.

'The French police seem to have worked it out,' said Lestrade. 'I'm sure it's just as they say. Mr Lucas' wife came on a surprise visit and he let her in. She told him she knew about his double life. The jealousy and anger overwhelmed her and she grabbed the first thing she saw: the curved dagger.

'There must have been a scuffle first though,' Lestrade went on, 'because the furniture was all over the place. And Mr Lucas must have used a chair to defend himself, because he was still holding it when we found him. I can imagine it as clearly as if I had seen it myself.'

Holmes raised his eyebrows. 'And yet you sent for me?'

'Ah, yes, that's another matter,' said Lestrade. 'Nothing

important, but just the sort of thing you'd be interested in. It's very strange.'

'What is it, then?' asked Holmes.

'Well, you know that after a crime has been committed we are very careful not to move anything. We need to see the evidence in the exact way the criminal left it. But this morning, now that the case is over, we decided to tidy up a bit.'

Inspector Lestrade pointed to the rug. 'We needed to lift this rug and when we did, we found ...'

Holmes' face grew tense and his fingers twitched with impatience.

'Well, I don't think you would guess in a hundred years what we found,' said Lestrade. 'You see that large bloodstain on the rug? Well, a lot of blood must have soaked through and onto the floor, don't you think?'

'Certainly,' said Holmes.

'You will be surprised to hear that there is no stain on the wooden floor underneath,' said Lestrade.

'No stain?' said Holmes.

'But that's impossible!' I said.

'You would think so.' Inspector Lestrade took a corner of the rug and lifted it up. 'But there isn't.' He chuckled with delight at having puzzled Holmes.

'There is a second stain,' Lestrade went on, 'but it doesn't line up with the one on the rug. See for yourself.'

He lifted up the opposite side of the rug and there, sure enough, was a big red stain on the wooden floor. 'What do you make of that, Mr Holmes?'

71

'Well, it's simple enough,' said Holmes as if it were obvious. 'The two stains did match, but the rug has been turned around. What I want to know is, who turned the rug and why?'

I could see from Holmes' face that excitement was

bubbling up inside of him. And there was only one reason Holmes would get so excited about such a simple thing – it was a clue to finding the stolen letter.

'Lestrade, has that constable been here all the time?'

Holmes asked, pointing towards the policeman standing outside the door.

'Yes, he has,' said Inspector Lestrade.

'Well, please ask him how he dared to let someone into this room and leave them alone,' Holmes snapped. 'Take him into another room. He is more likely to confess to you in private. Don't ask him *if* he did it. Tell him you *know* that someone has been in here. Someone has tampered with the scene of the crime.

Tell him that a confession is his only chance to save his job. Please do exactly as I tell you!'

'If he knows, I'll have it out of him!' said Inspector Lestrade. He dashed into the hallway and a few moments later his gruff voice sounded from the back room.

'Now, Watson, now!' cried Holmes. All the excitement burst out of Holmes in a spurt of energy. He peeled the rug from the floor and, in an instant, was down on his hands and knees clawing at each panel of wood.

'Help me, Watson,' he said, and I too fell to my knees and started clawing at the wooden floor. Finally, one panel moved as Holmes dug his nails into the edge of it. He lifted it up and it swung back on a hinge, like the

lid of a box. I could see a small black hole beneath it. Holmes plunged his hand into the hole, and then drew it back out with a snarl. It was empty.

'Quick, Watson, quick! Get it back again!' cried Holmes, when he heard Inspector Lestrade's voice in the passage, getting louder and louder as he approached the door.

Holmes shut the wooden lid and we placed the rug just as we had found it, seconds before Lestrade turned the door handle. As the inspector entered the room I was

standing on the rug and Holmes
was leaning casually against the
mantelpiece, pretending to yawn
with impatience.

'Sorry to keep you waiting, Mr Holmes,' said Inspector Lestrade. 'I can see that you are bored with this whole affair. Well, the constable has confessed all right. Come in here, MacPherson. Tell these gentlemen what you did.'

The constable looked flushed and very sorry for himself as he sidled into the room.

'I meant no harm, sir,' he said. 'The young woman came to the door yesterday evening. She said she had mistaken this house for another one, but we got talking.

It's lonely here all day on duty.'

'Well, what happened then?' asked Holmes.

'She wanted to see where the crime happened – she'd read about it in the newspaper. She was a very respectable young woman, sir, and I didn't see any harm in letting her have a peep. When she saw the bloodstain on the carpet, she fainted. I ran to the back room

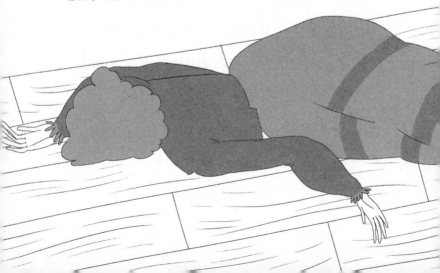

to get her some water but she still remained unconscious. I didn't know what to do, so I went to the pharmacy for some smelling salts, but by the time I got back the lady was gone. I expect she was embarrassed for fainting and didn't want to face me.'

'What about moving the rug?' asked Holmes.

'The rug, sir? I didn't move the rug,' said the constable, confused.

Holmes looked keenly from the constable to me, the sparks of an idea glinting in his eye.

'It's a lesson to you that you can't deceive me, MacPherson,' said Inspector Lestrade. 'You thought what you did would not be discovered, and yet just a glance at that rug told me that you had let someone come into the room. It's lucky for you, my man, that nothing is missing.'

I was about to say something, but Holmes placed his hand on my arm and smiled. He clearly didn't mind letting Lestrade take credit for his discovery.

Inspector Lestrade turned to

Holmes. 'I'm sorry to have called you over here for such a small thing, but I thought the fact that the second stain did not match the first one would interest you.'

'Certainly, it was most interesting,' said Holmes. 'Has this woman only been here once, constable?'

'Yes, sir, only once,' said the constable.

'Who was she?' asked Holmes.

'I don't know her name. She said she was answering an advertisement about a typewriting job, but came to the wrong house. She was a very pleasant young woman, sir.'

'Tall? Handsome?' asked Holmes.

'Yes, sir. And she was very persuasive. I really thought there was no harm in letting her just put her head through the door.' The constable looked down at his shoes and shook his head, ashamed.

'How was she dressed?' asked Holmes.

'She wore a long dress and gloves,' said the constable.

'And what time was it?' asked Holmes.

'Almost dusk,' said the constable. 'They were lighting the lamps in the street when I came back with the smelling salts.'

'Very good,' said Holmes. 'Come, Watson. I think that we have more important work elsewhere.'

Chapter Seven

The constable opened the door and let us out. Then Holmes turned on the step and held up something in his hand. I tried to peek over his shoulder, but couldn't see what it was.

The constable stared intently at the object in Holmes' hand. 'Good heavens, sir!' he cried in amazement.

Holmes put his finger to his lips and then replaced the item in his waistcoat pocket. As we turned down the street he burst out laughing.

'Excellent!' Holmes said. 'Come on, Watson, we are nearly at the end of this mystery. You will be glad to hear that there will be no war, and Mr Trelawney Hope will continue his brilliant career with no scandal.

'Plus, the writer of the letter will not be punished, and the prime minister won't have any problems in Europe to deal with. If we are careful, no one will be harmed by this ugly incident.'

'You have solved it?!' I cried.

'Almost. There are still some points that are unclear to me. We will go straight to Whitehall Terrace and put the final pieces of the puzzle together.'

When we arrived at the foreign minister's house, Holmes asked to see his wife, Lady Hope. We were shown into the drawing room, where she was seated at a writing desk.

'Mr Holmes!' Lady Hope sprang to her feet, her face pink with anger. 'It is most unfair of you to come here. I asked you to keep my visit to Baker Street a secret. And now you come here, showing that we have a business arrangement.'

'There was nothing else I could do, Madam,' said Holmes. 'I have been asked to find this important letter. Please be kind enough to give it to me.'

Lady Hope's face went pale. She staggered a bit and I thought

she might faint. Then she took
a big breath and shouted, 'You
insult me, Mr Holmes!'

'Please, Lady Hope. Give up the
letter,' said Holmes.

She darted to the bell-pull, her
hand hovering threateningly over

the tasselled end. 'The butler will show you out.'

'Do not ring, Lady Hope,' said Holmes. 'If you do then you will spoil all my efforts to avoid scandal. Give up the letter and everything will be all right. If you will work with me, I can arrange everything.'

Lady Hope's eyes were fixed on Holmes' as if she were trying to read his mind. Then, after a moment, her hand fell from the bell-pull.

'You are trying to frighten me, Mr Holmes,' she said. 'It's not kind.

You say you know something. So what is it that you know?'

'Please sit down, Madam, and I will tell you,' said Holmes. 'I will not speak until you sit.'

She did so and said, 'I will give you five minutes, Mr Holmes.'

'One is enough, Lady Hope,' said Holmes. 'I know of your visit to Mr Eduardo Lucas. I know you gave him the secret letter and that you returned to his room last night and took the letter back from Mr Lucas' hiding place under the rug.'

Lady Hope stared at Holmes with a pale face and gulped twice before she could speak.

'You are mad, Mr Holmes,' she said at last.

Holmes took a small piece of cardboard from his pocket. I could see that it was the face of a woman cut out of a portrait.

'I carried this because I thought it might be useful,' said Holmes, holding it out in front of her. 'The constable recognised it.'

She gasped.

'Come, Lady Hope. You have the letter. We can still put this right. I don't want to bring you any trouble. My duty ends when I have returned the lost letter to your husband. Take my advice and be honest with me. It is your only chance.'

'I tell you again, Mr Holmes, that you are mistaken,' she said.

I had to admire Lady Hope's courage. Even now she would not give up. Holmes got up from his chair. 'Then I am sorry, Lady Hope,' he said. 'I have done my best for you, but I can see that it was all for nothing.'

Holmes rang the bell and the butler entered.

'Is Mr Hope at home?' asked Holmes.

'He will be home at quarter to one, sir,' said the butler.

Holmes pulled out his pocket watch and glanced at it. 'Fifteen

minutes,' he said. 'Never mind.
I shall wait.'

The butler had hardly closed
the door behind him when Lady
Hope fell onto her knees at
Holmes' feet. Her hands were
outstretched and her face was wet
with tears.

Chapter Eight

'Oh, please, Mr Holmes, don't tell my husband!' Lady Hope pleaded. 'I love him so much. I do not want to cause him pain. This would break his noble heart!'

'Thank goodness you have come to your senses,' said Holmes, helping her up again. 'Where is the letter? There is not a moment to lose!'

Lady Hope darted across to the writing desk, unlocked its drawer, and took out a long blue envelope.

'Here it is, Mr Holmes. I wish I had never seen it,' she said.

'How can we return it? Quick, we must think of a way!' said Holmes, a little flustered. 'Where is your husband's box? The one he locked the letter in before it was stolen.'

'Still in his bedroom,' Lady Hope said.

'What a stroke of luck,' said
Holmes. 'Quick, madam, bring
it here.'

Lady Hope dashed out of the
room and a moment later, came
back with a flat red box in her
hand.

'How did you open it before?
Do you have a key?' asked
Holmes.

Lady Hope reached for a chain
around her neck. On the end
of it was a small key, which she

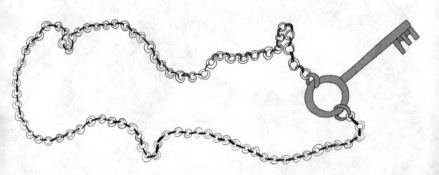

inserted into the keyhole of the box. The red lid sprang open.

The box was stuffed with papers. Holmes thrust the blue envelope deep down into the heart of them, between some other

documents, before snapping the lid shut. Lady Hope locked the box and returned it to the bedroom.

'Now we are ready for him,' said Holmes. 'And with ten minutes to spare. Well done us!'

Holmes glanced at Lady Hope's worried face. 'Do not panic, Lady Hope, I will protect your secret. But you must tell me the truth about what happened.'

'I will tell you everything,' said Lady Hope.

'Good. Do so quickly. There's not much time left,' said Holmes.

'It all started with a letter I wrote to a gentleman I hardly knew,' Lady Hope began, her words tripping over one another in the race to be spoken. 'A horrible, foolish love letter, written before I was married. I was a thoughtless, silly girl. I meant no harm, but if my husband read it, his respect for me would be destroyed forever.'

Sadness and worry painted themselves across Lady Hope's face, turning her once-pretty smile into a tearful frown. My heart went out to her.

'I heard that this man, Mr Lucas, had my letter and was going to give it to my husband,' she continued. 'I begged him not to. He said he would give me back my letter if I brought him a certain document that was locked in my husband's paperwork box. Mr Lucas promised me that no harm would come to my husband. What was I to do, Mr Holmes?'

'You could have told your husband about it,' said Holmes. I silently agreed with him.

'I could not, Mr Holmes. He would never have understood. It was terrible to take the letter from my husband's box, but I promise I had no idea how important it was.' Lady Hope paused and wiped a tear from her cheek.

'What happened at Godolphin Street, when you took the letter to Mr Lucas?' asked Holmes.

'I tapped on the door as agreed,' she said. 'Mr Lucas opened it. I followed him into his sitting room, but left the door open as I was afraid to be alone with him. There was a woman standing outside as I entered.

'Our business was soon done. I handed him the long blue envelope and he gave me my letter. At that moment, there was a sound from outside. Mr Lucas quickly flung back

the rug, tucked the blue letter into a hiding place in the floor, and covered it over again.'

Lady Hope's face drained of colour. 'What happened after that is like a nightmare. The woman from outside stormed in and began screaming in French, "At last I have found you with her!" Then there was a struggle. I saw Mr Lucas with a chair in his hand, and the woman grabbed a curved knife from the wall. I was so scared that I ran away. The next morning, I read in the newspaper about what happened.'

Holmes glanced at the clock above the fireplace and waved his hand for Lady Hope to carry on. Mr Hope was due back at any moment – we were running out of time.

'I soon realised that I had swapped one problem for another,' she continued. 'My husband was so sad about losing the blue letter that I almost told him what I had done. Then, after I discovered how important the letter was, I was determined to get it back. I thought it must still be where Mr Lucas hid it under the rug.

'I watched the house for two days, but the door was never left open. Then, last night I decided I must get in somehow, so I tricked the police constable into letting me in. I found the hidden letter and brought it back with me, but I didn't know how I could return it to him … Oh no! I hear him coming!'

Chapter Nine

Mr Hope burst excitedly into the room. 'Do you have any news, Mr Holmes?'

'There is hope,' said Holmes.

'Ah! Thank goodness!' His face lit up. 'The prime minister is downstairs. May he share your hopes? I know he has hardly slept since this affair began.'

Holmes nodded and Mr Hope

called to the butler. 'Jacobs, please ask the prime minister to come up. As to you, my dear,' he said to Lady Hope, 'this is a matter of politics. We will join you in a few minutes in the dining room.'

The prime minister was quiet as he entered the room. 'I understand that you have something to report, Mr Holmes?' he said.

'Nothing positive yet,' said Holmes. 'But I am certain of one thing – the letter has not gone into the wrong hands.'

'But that is not enough, Mr Holmes!' said the prime minister. 'We cannot just cross our fingers and hope for the best. We need to know where it is and who has it.'

'The more I think about it, the more sure I am that the letter never left this house,' said Holmes.

'Mr Holmes!' cried Mr Hope. 'What a silly idea. Of course it left the house.'

Holmes shook his head. 'If it had left, it would have been made public by now.'

'But why should anyone steal the letter just to keep it in this house?' asked the prime minister.

'I am not sure that anyone did steal it,' said Holmes.

'Then how could it have left my box?' snapped Mr Hope.

'I am not sure that it ever did leave your box,' said Holmes.

'Mr Holmes, this is no time to joke! It certainly did leave the box!' shouted Mr Hope, now losing his patience.

'Have you looked in the box since Tuesday morning?' asked Holmes.

'No.'

'Then you may have missed it,' said Holmes calmly.

'Impossible, Mr Holmes!'

'I have known such things to happen,' said Holmes. 'I assume there are other papers in there? It could have been mixed up with them.'

Mr Hope shook his head. 'It was on top.'

The prime minister interrupted. 'Surely, this can easily be checked, Mr Hope. Let us have the box brought in.'

Mr Hope rang the bell.

'Jacobs,' he said to the butler, 'please bring in my paperwork box.'

The butler brought it in and placed it on the table.

'This is a complete waste of time,' said Mr Hope, pulling out the key from a chain around his neck, just as his wife had done. He unlocked the box and opened it.

'See, here is a letter from Lord Merrow and a report from Sir Charles Hardy,' he said. 'Here are some notes from Belgrade and one about the Russian grain taxes.'

Mr Hope rummaged about in the box, pulling out the papers and putting them on the table beside the box.

'There's a note from Lord
Flowers and … good heavens!
What is this? Prime Minister!
Prime Minister!'

The prime minister snatched the blue envelope from Mr Hope. 'Yes, this is it! And it hasn't been opened! Mr Holmes, I congratulate you!'

'But this is impossible,' said Mr Hope, astounded. 'Mr Holmes, you are a wizard! How did you know it was there?'

'Because I knew it was nowhere else,' said Holmes.

'I cannot believe my eyes,' said Mr Hope. He ran to the door. 'Where is my wife? I must tell her that all is well. Hilda! Hilda!'

We heard his voice on the stairs.

The prime minister looked at Holmes with twinkling eyes. 'There is more to this than meets the eye, isn't there, Mr Holmes? How did the letter get back into the box?'

Holmes turned away, smiling.
'We all have our secrets,' he said.
Then he picked up his hat and we
headed for the door.

'A wizard, eh?' I said as we
walked back to Baker Street.
'You'll be pulling rabbits out of
hats next!'

Holmes threw back his head
and laughed.

Sherlock Holmes

World-renowned private detective Sherlock Holmes has solved hundreds of mysteries, and is the author of such fascinating monographs as *Early English Charters* and *The Influence of a Trade Upon the Form of a Hand*. He keeps bees in his free time.

Dr John Watson

Wounded in action at Maiwand, Dr John Watson left the army and moved into 221B Baker Street. There he was surprised to learn that his new friend, Sherlock Holmes, faced daily peril solving crimes, and began documenting his investigations. Dr Watson also runs a doctor's practice.

To download Sherlock Holmes activities, please visit
www.sweetcherrypublishing.com/resources